Papers from the Steps of Battelle

By Matthew Craig

First Edition
March 2013

Portions of this book were originally published as independent works.

Published by Junkhouse Entertainment
www.junkhouseentertainment.com

Printed in the United States of America

To my Father on his birthday.
Two birds with one stone.

Table of Contents:

Foreword

Papers from the Steps of Battelle is a collection of my works from 2003 to late 2010. Though predominately short fiction, there are experiments with poetry, philosophy, humanism, and song lyrics as well.

During the time period of my life represented by these works, I struggled through college (attending first American University and then George Mason University), fell in love many times, and contended every day with self identification in the swirling seas of humanity. Battelle-Tompkins was one of the many, many buildings I occupied.

Perhaps published for publishing's sake, *Papers from the Steps of Battelle* is for me akin to an archeological dig site, preserving what endured through my twenties. I wanted to release it back when the work was current, but in all honesty I panicked (as all writers must do), immersed in fears that these collected works would characterize my thirties and define the rest of my life.

One month before my thirty-first birthday, all the bullshit about uncertainty (and receptiveness of a work like this in the literary community) finally wore off.

It is what it is.

Our Hero

Our hero sat there, under the overhang, between the buildings. Rain poured down. Across the way he could see his reflection in a window. There was a girl too, sitting near him. But looking at her in the window across the way, she seemed far away, too far to reach.

The reflections were pale, translucent figures that seemed to be floating. The rain kept falling, more movement between the buildings, more figures reflected in the window.

The universe grew and grew until our hero was lost on the wrong side of the window. He sat there and thought about what to do, but the peace and strange symmetry of the situation brought him apathy.

His eyes rolled and he slumped over, fast asleep. Darkness washed over him, and somewhere out in the black oblivion, a little voice was heard to say, "…is that guy ok?"

Mr. Mugger and My Rolex Watch

Yeah, so the gun was to my head. Actually, the barrel was pressed against my temple. I had given him my wallet and gotten pistol-whipped. For my watch, I got a knee in the face.

And when on the ground with a broken nose I growled out, "What the fuck else do you want?!?" – I was the proud recipient of a well-placed kick to the ribs. As I lay there in fair amounts of pain, I could hear that bastard running off with my fifteen dollars and my fake Rolex.

The money was nothing and the watch was even less. The only thing taken that I really cared about was a wallet sized picture of one of my old girlfriends. My thoughts drifted to her as I picked myself up off the ground. I tried to imagine what it would be like for her to turn the corner and see me standing there with a busted face and sore ribs.

My head was pounding. I needed a drink.

Through blurred vision I saw her small frame coming toward me. I could barely make out her long brown hair. When she was mine I had always worshiped her feminine curves and that silky brown hair that reached all the way down to the small of her back.

Even when she put it up or braided it, she still had me. I called her my "blue eyed angel", and when I told her I loved her, I meant it.

I knew she wasn't really there. What I saw in that alley was a phantom. I saw exactly what I wanted to see. I wanted her to come up to me and hug me. Hug me like she thought she had lost me forever. I wanted to tell her about the empty part of me where she used to be. But there was nothing there and I was acting like a fool.

It started to rain. As I walked out of the alley, I came across my wallet. Mr. Mugger must have decided he didn't want it after all. He had taken the money, but he had left her faded picture.

(late 2003)

Untitled

Some days, I am king of the world. And other times I am king of nothing and have little say inside me.

I can be impervious and I can be fragile. This is not unique to me; I am not singularly a recipient of doubt or pride.

(2004)

Shadows and Spirits

It's been two years since I last saw her. Two years and five months since we last made love. It's hard to keep track of these things. Two years and eleven months since she thought she was pregnant. Three years and some days since we decided to love each other for as long as we could stand it.

To be honest, I will never stop counting the days as they pass. The flip side of the coin is that I know she is never coming back. Where does Romanticism meet pathetic compulsion? Am I a sucker for a pretty face, or am I one of the few left on this rock that comprehends the beauty of the most personal and intimate of relationships? There is no way for me to answer these questions. The outside in approach is the only way. Fresh eyes belonging to new people I meet. Let them decide for themselves.

To continue to be honest, I don't think I really care too much about what others might think. The questions I pose are more for my own reflection. She is gone, and the acknowledgment I have given is more than the relationship ever deserved. Love places very heavy weights on me.

In my last gasp of juvenile delight, I'd like to admit that I will love her forever. It doesn't cost anything, and the snapshot memories are simply not worth throwing away.

(June 2004)

Well Haunted

Let me paint you a picture. Life seems fine and though it may not be your best of days, it's certainly no bitch. Night falls and suddenly you find that the ground you happen to be standing on is some sort of magnet for ghosts. This ground can be anything, a gas station, nightclub, or even your own kitchen (trust me on this one). These aren't just any ghosts but real people from your past.

Confidentially, I call them "ghosts" because they are people I have cared for deeply but who chose to evacuate from my life, move on, and pass me by, whatever. It's when they show up for no good reason, long after you personally declare them legally dead, that these very real humans attain their ethereal status. You're being haunted, visited from beyond. Ghosts.

So there you are and life seems fine, but then without the slightest warning... the spirit parade begins. Whether it's a Mr. or a Ms., the shock and crushing wave of feeling is all the same. It buries you up to your neck and they get to watch. If you had even a year's worth of abandonment by this person, you've probably had plenty of time to think up something awful to say. A barrage of cute insults and comebacks to counter with sit quietly, waiting in your pocket. The irony being, you had given them up as lost by now and figured you'd never have to use them. Cold War relics.

Worst case scenario: they appear magically in front of you, out of thin air. Ghosts don't appear in kitchens huh? I saw one. I was getting water from the fridge and when I turned around, she was there. We are talking about four or five months of no contact. I had loved this one a lot too. That's what creates the most powerful ones.

It wasn't that a catastrophe happened to keep us from talking, it was just that neither bothered to try. I sank and she just kept on swimming. Now though, she was going to be the bad guy and I was going to prove it with logic most skillful, backed up by the malice only a jilted lover could provide. But everyone knows: you can't hurt ghosts.

I was totally disarmed. There was no great battle, no one-sided tongue lashing either. This nasty "turn around type" surprise scrambled my brain in the time it took for me to swallow.

I hadn't seen her since she had decided to leave me. In sector G-259 something, the ex-girlfriend department of my brain (an old dusty place in the basement), the harried clerk just grabbed the first stack of files with her name that he could find and sent them on to the main office. The stack didn't contain the launch codes for the insults.

In it, instead, were memories. Those memories had the word KEEP stamped on them, containing basically whatever happy memories I had managed to salvage from the anger stage. There were even a few that I could never throw away. All I could be was passive; I couldn't hurt her with my words, couldn't attack the co-creator of those memories. I couldn't.

When you factor in love, the Don of the emotional crime family, the other side of any equation seems to be reduced to zero by its magnitude. This is a thesis I'm working on. I've been hard at this one for more years than ten. Though I may be lying.

My anger and hate for her treatment was tempered by the fact that she had disappeared and reappeared so suddenly, all I could remember was love. The shock as I said had also done its bit of work.

I was defenseless but I was lucky. She had come in peace to see how I was; it was all about good intentions. A last check-up to make sure the "separation surgery" healed in a fair way. I didn't attack and she was made to comfortable. I was a good post-op patient.

In so far as ghosts go, she haunted me well that late afternoon for at least two hours.

There were some tears from her and some heavy sighs from me. I asked her to stay, I was being silly. Then she disappeared out my door. Ghosts use doors sometimes. That was a long time ago, seems like it anyway. I wonder if she will haunt me again someday. I wonder if she will be as powerful. I've seen a lot of ghosts.

Reality Check

Reality check. This is a test of the emergency broadcast system. This is only a test. Had this been anything more than a dry run, then you would have to agree that as far as performances go, it sucked. And you weren't ready.

Facts:

I am not, nor ever will be, more than a single entity.

I do not enjoy (in its *Entirety*). It is a relative inconvenience.

If I am missing parts to a whole, I did not start with them to begin with.

I am only aware of the passage of time relative to my life. This is to say that my time is the only time that can be considered real through experiential determination.

When I can not understand something I get angry.

(2004)

Untitled

Daisy chain adult fuck-fest go!

Ready the Cannons!

Prepare to Fire!

God pains those who forget to make reservations at the last supper restaurant because it's really packed in there and the wait time on a good table for four at the dinner hour is so fucking ridiculous – that I'm going to take my bitch of a girlfriend down to Hardees if she doesn't shut the fuck up. God, I hate her friends.

This is me. Who am I? Fucking retard of a day dreamer- and eat me very much. I will mix candy flavored words with 100 proof confusion and blend daiquiris of alliteration for you – but I will kick your ass smooth out of this place if you get drunk and nasty with me, bar fly. Yeah, I called you that. Because here, in my mind, you are a bar fly. A know nothing. A tourist. So, what's on tap for today, tourist? You wanna see some monuments?

They all do.

Untitled

I loved you so much, I mourned your disappearance like it was your death. I loved you so much that it scared me that it took so little time to fall in love.

I loved you so much I wanted to ask you to marry me after our first real night together – but I loved you so much that I couldn't gamble like that.

Back and Forth, Too and Fro

I've discovered a way to travel in time. It isn't for sale. I won't teach it. I can only imagine what the general population would do with the knowledge. Perhaps others already travel as freely as I do... If that's the case, I don't need to tell anyone anyway.

I can still remember when I first traveled out of the present and into the future. I went too far, past my lifespan. I witnessed the world without me in it.

Crazy Jonny

Look there's Jonny, what's he gonna do?
He may hurt me or he may hurt you.
The guy's got a gun and he's crazy as a loon.
If they're gonna lock him up then they'd better do it soon.
I heard he once caught his friend with his wife –
and he shot'em both up in the middle of the night.
He cut'em into pieces and mailed'em to the cops, -
particularly the wife's head with those pretty golden locks.

Richmond is for Lovers

Try having a friend who's a junkie. Try knowing someone who may have an exceptional skill hidden inside, but who can't seem to break to manifested chemical dependence on heroin. See if you can guess what it's like. No wait. Go out and make friends with a junkie. It's good for life experience if you're into that sort of thing, good for the soul if you have strong ties to any sort of religion and you believe that helping others find salvation means you yourself will attain salvation.

Don't make it a family member, the natural inclination will be to pity and feel sorrow for a "lost" member of your tree. Whomever you choose to be your junkie, there must be no connection in the order of family. The feelings you feel must not be obligatory.

Try to find someone who isn't a junkie yet but fits the prospective profile (whatever the hell that is). It will be a much more informative and educational experience if you can observe the transition from capable human being to shambling smack monkey.

It will help test all the feelings in your vanilla folder of emotions.

Be careful not to get too attached to your field study, as you will inevitably become mired in the bantering politics of withdrawal sickness versus kicking the H - a stunning series of illogical conclusions and balderdash theories that make a non-users head swim. You see, a junkie's eyes sparkle at the possibility of talking about his situation, and the drugs.

So go out and get yourself a junkie of a smack addict or an H-user or a dope fiend and experience for yourself the joy of having them chew on your soul.

There are college courses for everything else, why not teach this subject? Talk to your local congressman about it. We can call it: “Sociological decay in the Twentieth Century with direct correlations to habitual drug users.”

Creationism

You can create ghosts as easily as they manifest themselves. In fact, it is fact, that these particular kinds of ghosts are the ones you are most likely to attempt to make contact with. Your creative force powers the tie that binds.

It may be greedy to assume that you have the right, but it is still heroic to confront a ghost. In this new century there are no genuine heroes.

(late 2005)

On the Most Beautiful Monday Morning I Can Remember

It takes a lot to make a man do the things I did. I loved this girl once. Let's call her Leanne for the purposes of this story. One day she up and disappeared on me. Or, she thought she did.

For two years I kept open channels on the street and occasionally, I would come upon a credible piece of information regarding her whereabouts. I never followed those leads. Not because I didn't want to either.

More because her life was her own and she must have left me for something I couldn't give her. It took a lot of will power to accept that.

By the third year I was done looking for her and back to just plain looking. Time of course moves along with all of us on board, we just don't all sit together. And in that time she had met a bad man and had a beautiful baby girl. Let's call her Jillian for the purposes of this story.

Of course, he went to jail for 20 years or something (I never gave a damn enough to remember) and she was stuck in a well. This is America.

Five or so years of separate lives ended when she used My Space to find a mutual friend. Calling me was next. I knew when she was going to call and I got drunk in a precipitous manner much as a soldier who fears his first battle might.

It prepared me to do or say whatever I had to in order to get by. It didn't help but it didn't hurt either. To tell you the truth I really don't recall anything I said. But I am sure I mentioned love.

I tried to write her a letter but her family intercepted it. Talking to her on the phone was not something she was really supposed to be doing. She had married that bad man and was living with his family. Where does morality make you hit the brakes?

I understand that here I should have moved along. This was trouble no doubt. But something in me failed to care enough about the sanctity of marriage (or any other social convention) and in this I must better explain...

At 26 I had been in some sort of school system for more than 88.5% of my life rounding up, I did the math. If there was a system I wasn't familiar with you can bet someone was going to tell me I needed to attend a course on it just to graduate.

While jumping through hoops, people were always asking me what I was going to do with a history degree.

Apparently, everyone not getting a history degree already knows:

You simply can't get good work anywhere (and by good I mean $40,000+/a year). I hated bureaucracy and I was being groomed for it. I hated adults and the decisions they made; and I was becoming one more and more every day. I was learning how to sit in someone else's office and wait for them to double check my figures with someone in another office far, far away.

Sometimes when people asked me what I was going to do I said I was going to steal a large boat from a rich person and sail the world with it until I found a place where I could live. I never said "...happily ever after", but you get the idea.

I had it all figured out. Rich people can't be bothered with maps. Every large sea worthy vessel has a Global Positioning System. That tidy piece of gear could take me anywhere.

If I could collect enough money to buy enough supplies to get me across the ocean, I'd be able to make a home somewhere and maybe go back for anything else. Maybe.

People always gave me two very predictable responses:
1. "Sounds nice. I hope it works out."
2. "Good luck Gilligan."

I ignored those second category jerks as best I could. Girlfriends always fell into saying the first category but you could tell that deep inside, they were second category all the way.

Leanne was the exception to the rule. Way back when - I had told her about this pipe dream and she said, "When you're ready to go, call me because I'm going too." I loved her just for that. But when she said that she was 17 and I was 21 and we still had some life to live before we bailed on everybody and everything.

By the time of my 26th birthday I had collected more than $9,000 in an online bank account that I hadn't told anybody about. Birthday and Christmas money, drug money, odd-job money, and a little college loan money that should have been spent on books and other things; it was all there and in my mind it would be enough.

I started reading books on sailing, riggings, weather patterns, marine life, anything. Red sky at night, sailor's delight; red sky at morning, sailor's warning. I also had gone to several harbor and marine storage sites to look things over.

It started as a general curiosity I had to entertain, but when I found a particular marina that had only two guys on night security (a white guy and a black guy I had affectionately named Nose-picker and

Snoozer) and a not so secure front gate, that became the place I would sail from. Several times I skirted in and wandered the grounds after hours while they watched a little television they had in the guard house. Just a few weeks before Leanne reappeared I had picked out a beautiful 200ft schooner-type yacht. She was called the Swingin' Judge and she was perfect.

I spent a little time aboard her. I even eventually started talking to her quietly to myself. There were sleeping quarters, a food prep area, generators, a satellite phone, and even scuba gear for four people.

The boat was owned by a real old-fashioned Hater of Men named Judge Franklin Crandall Stempson. Friends and enemies alike called him "Swingin' Stempson" because of his proclivity for recommending the death penalty in almost any case that would allow it.

His father had been a judge in Chicago in the 60's and 70's when hippies and civil rights agitators needed to be “put in their place and made to be nothing but a foot note in history”, and his father had been a judge in Washington D.C. in the 50’s and 40’s when suspected communist agents and left-wing Hollywood types needed to be “rooted out and snuffed out with a patriotic fervor that would make the founding fathers seem like fair weather Americans.”

I, of course knew nothing about all this. I just wanted his boat.

Stempson had a GPS system, and a nice one at that. Insurance would pay the man right? When the time came I would buy hotdogs and kerosene. Crackers and canned food too. Maybe some bait for the deep sea fishing poles that were on the Judge.

The Judge had a deep freezer. I needed to buy lumber and a few tools from a store. I would also need piping for irrigation and farming. It all had to be paid for in cash and I couldn’t afford a storage site.

Everything would have to be purchased inside a single day and put on board that night (I would sail early that next morning). It would be a surprise attack.

By the time I was deemed missing and the boat was reported too, I planned to be well off the coast of the continental U.S. and there would be nothing anyone could do about it. I even had a special plan for the two security guards since I was sure they weren't going to help me load up for the trip or wave goodbye.

I had never really planned to take anybody with me. I was going to have to become almost instantly self-sufficient. I had to build a shelter and fish until I could farm.

I don't even like fish, but I would learn. I took me a while to build up the personal courage to want to go it alone. People aren't supposed to sail alone for safety reasons. It was fate I believe, that gave me a chance to ask Leanne if she and Jillian wanted to go with me.

I understand that asking the wife of another man to run away with you is wrong, but he wasn't going to be around to love her and her baby for a long time. Besides, I was going with or without her.

We e-mailed back and forth a while until I felt comfortable enough to spring the idea on her. She decided to pack up Jillian and go with me. Much later, some people would still say I kidnapped them but there were no signs of forced entry at the house.

I still laugh at the ogre-ish depiction of me by the boys at FOX and MSNBC. I can't or won't examine the real reasons that she had for deciding to come with me.

On the most beautiful Monday morning I can remember, I went to where she and Jillian were staying and picked the two of them up in a white Ford dually-modified pickup that I had "borrowed" from my friend's father. By 2:00 pm I had three helpers in orange vests loading my goods at Home Depot. I even bought a can of marine based oil paint to rename our boat.

Something about those vests made me shiver and Leanne saw it. She took my hand and said, “We need to get going.” By 6:00 pm we had purchased 28 bags of groceries and 15 gallons of water.

On the way to the marina Leanne had to hold Jillian in her lap and we could barely see each other over the bags and piping. We caught a radio report about us. I was a thief and a maniac and she was my victim. Leanne giggled a little. A tiny person inside me was trying to get me to stop the truck and that giggle killed him dead.

The marina entrance was off the main road a way and Leanne sat behind the wheel of the truck while I went down to the gate to slip in and deal with the boys at the guard house. There was a fuse box on the outside of the booth and I crept up to it and cut the power. I had rehearsed this in my mind a thousand times but my fingers were cold and numb from anxiety as I pulled the switch.

Blackness upset those trolls and out they came. Snoozer was immediately maced and Nose-picker hesitated, guaranteeing the same for him. While they coughed and cried, I flexi-cuffed them together.

I opened the gate and went up to bring the truck through. The sight of the guards upset Leanne a little but I reassured her they would be alright. All night they jabbered on and on about how we were in so much trouble and about how they knew us from the T.V.

By 9:00 am the Swingin' Judge was ready to sail. Before taking up the mooring lines, I maced the guards one more time and then cut them free. They could call whoever the hell they wanted to now.

We went down the coast of Virginia and out into the Atlantic. Two days out to sea I was in love with her again and I was in love with little Jillian too. How they became my fictive wife and daughter so fast, I'll never understand. We rechristened the Judge the Escape Pod and decided we were from

Australia (we took down the American flag and gave it a proper burial at sea and I produced an Aussie flag out of my backpack). I thought we were home free but four days at sea and just east of Savannah GA, Jillian developed an ear infection and a fever.

This was the first time Leanne was really worried, and it was also the first time we slept in the same cabin at night. That was also the first night I really wanted to go home and give up on my dreams.

I sailed without sleep for a day and a half to the Gulf of Mexico and came into Okaloosa, Florida for help. I had a grandmother there and other family as well. We came in at night and gave her a nasty shock. We were all over the national news now.

The truck had been found intact and undamaged. Plus the two families concerned were now being deluged with reporters and police. We spent three days there waiting for Jillian to get better and finally we were ready to leave. In that time however, people had found us and were closing in quickly. My grandmother, trying to do the right thing, had called my mother on day three. My mother had contacted my father, and my father had notified the police.

Soon Leanne's family knew too, and they were on their way. In the back of this mad procession down to Florida was the man they called Swingin' Stempson.

As we were eating breakfast, the distinct sound of justice came roaring into the driveway. I grabbed a chair and cinched up the door but it was a stall. Leanne picked up Jillian and we bolted out the sliding glass door and into the back yard, down the steps and racing toward the dock, trying desperately to get to the boat and get it moving.

I stopped to untie the mooring lines as she jumped aboard and took Jillian. My fingers were fumbling, "why now?" There was a loud ringing in my ears and I heard Jillian crying.

I heard Leanne say she loved me and was screaming at me not to go.

“Where would I go”, I said, “Where would I go without you?”

(early 2005)

Untitled

I think it's Wednesday. I don't know for sure. I don't even really care.

Days are failing to register. System error.

Untitled

Thought work for most is a grocery list, or a series of extraneous farts, that have to be farted in such a way as to not offend everyone around. You're going to fart. Why the hell is there finesse to it?

For me it (thought work) is an endless parade of faces and words. Thoughts of all types push me down and call me an EXPLETIVE DELETED.

Now I'm being censored.

What the fuck am I trying to say?

(2005)

I’ve Been Thinking

I’ve been thinking for awhile now of stealing about and sailing away from American in the hopes of finding a better place. Maybe boat isn’t a big enough word. Yaght? Yacht? A bigger boat that the word boat can convey. How fucking hard can it be to sail anyway?

I’ve tried to discuss all this with others but any average Joe would be just as likely to laugh as to say good luck. I’m leaving because people are always “just as likely”.

The moral conflict of stealing isn’t strong since I’m gonna need a big boat and only rich people have those. Stealing from the rich is a kinky turn-on. Eat chocolate cake frosting with taco shells, fuck in the shower, and steal from the rich.

I’m just as likely to become a convicted felon as to successfully pull off a boat heist of this magnitude.

(early 2006)

Who Needs This Shit ?

Where's my parachute, I'm getting' the hell off this ride. Y'all can go down with the ship. Hell, you are the ship. Who needs this shit? If I had my way, I'd kill a billion people every day.

(2006)

School Dance

"College ain't for me", he said as he tossed
his books on the floor.

"I'd rather nibble on a shotgun instead."
- as he waltzed right out the door.

Gin with a Stork Chaser

I can remember a white beach at night. A quiet beach means wildlife. I can remember these white Herons playing in the surf. They came close. I was a quiet drunk. Those wild birds brought a strange peace to me.

“Gin with a stork chaser please.”

“I got a long way to go, might as well dull the mind if I can’t numb the feet.”

(summer 2006)

Untitled

24yo. seeks nexus that leads to alternate universe. Enjoys long walks, watching movies, and fantasizing about altered physical properties of matter in an excited state.

Degradation Gratification

Man is in man's way. Man is holding up man's progress. What kind of mathematical problem always leads to negation?

Is it possible that "No man is an island"' is a misnomer?

If man was an island, I'm living at the moment of Pangaea and the moment never passes. An infinite amount of mass pushing and shoving their way across the earth. Analyze my handwriting, see if it explains my desire to separate and float away.

My bandwagon is a one man rocket sled with racing stripes and a shiny red button in the cockpit that says: Do not push, EVER. My bandwagon comes equipped with an ejection seat and I come equipped with a parachute, a moral parachute that says: I'm HUMAN, when it deploys.

So, humanity's an excuse huh? I could attempt to sit in the same place for a thousand years but somewhere along the line of time, someone is going to want to occupy my place.

(2006)

Untitled

"I'm not saying we should burn down the system. I'm saying that human beings have never been able to maintain an ordered system for long. A few thousand years? If they lasted a millennia maybe I'd give'em a sniff. Until then guy…"

It's all awry.

A house of cards on a teeter-totter with glass ball bearings, that's what I see. Besides, if humans were meant to live in a cage (real or intangible) they wouldn't have evolved from wild animals.

(2006)

Misanthrope

I hate,

every living thing.

From the birds, to the bees that sting.

But it's people that I hate most of all, from
the short and fat – to skinny and tall.

Y'all should have to fight in a cage with
swords, spiked pits, and flames.

It's easy to hate people you see – 'cause I'm
a misanthrope and happy to be.

(2006)

That's That

There are so many people in the world today
who'd punch you in the face if you said,
"You may."

And they'd bend you over, and they'd have
their way.

And they ache at the chance just to drag you
away…

It ain't what you say, no it's who you know.

And if you don't like yourself babe it really
shows.

And if you wear those weights and act that
way, then the scum of the earth – well,
they'll smell you like prey and that…

well that's that.

Spilling Your Guts

When you want to tell someone about everything you think, do you recognize the possible direct and disastrous consequences?

Humans can be at times a little predatory to say the least. Predators determine "potential" from signs of weakness, and telling another human all about yourself or what's going on has been referred to as "spilling your guts".

Predators eat guts most of the time.

How do you spill your guts? I'm asking you. Do you? Everyone's bursting at the seams with stuff that they feel sets them apart and thereby isolates them a little more.

People feel better when they share commonality, including the awareness department. I want to spill my guts. I damn sure will too. Watch me catapult back into the heart of society from the fringes by getting "it" off my chest.

But when my guts come out I am dead. Or if not dead, surely close to it. Let's all isolate ourselves a little more, or start spilling. And let that be the strongest dividing line between men.

(2007)

Immunity Tree

Where to begin?

If there was a beginning, it was somewhere in Arlington. At least, that's the first place I can remember. I used to hide under a pine tree next to the house. You could see the whole street, parking lot too.

Under that tree, superheroes battled powerful evil on a constant basis. Sometimes, I figured I was invisible. I could witness the workings of the whole world with universal immunity. That tree is gone now. I haven't felt immune for a long time.

(2007)

The Morality of Funding

"Which way to the exit?", if you can believe the possibility of escape? A young man can feel incredibly trapped. But the word trapped implies prior freedom.

"No, no…something else."

A young man can feel quite worthless at times in an age of mass communication and buying power. "Is this really all there is?"

If a time machine can get me out, is it morally wrong to steal to get the funding?

"Which way to the door?" I don't want to operate under glass anymore.

(Fall 2007)

Go away, Go away

Little girl, who once rocked my world –

Here now you sigh, with a baby on your thigh
but it ain't mine. So now I start to cry. 'Cause
now I see just what I could have been.

And by the way,

if you could go back from where you came
(that'd be great)

Please try today 'cause can't you see you're
driving me insane.

Junkie kid, whom I once called my friend –

The day you died, I knew I hadn't tried to save
your life. And now I wonder why. A curse you
fool, that's all your death did to me!

And by the way,

if you could go back from where you came
(that'd be great)

Please try today 'cause can't you see you're
driving me insane.

(2007)

Days Like These

I'm still going. I have to admit, sometimes I'm splitting wide open at the seams. The sick insanity comes oozing out. Sometimes I feel incredibly sexual. I want to demonstrate my sexual prowess for (to) each pretty girl I see. I want to get off on getting them off.

I must be some kind of animal. Days like these convince me of it. Vanitus Animalius.

(2007)

"Baby its cold outside"

Stupid Super Powers Ain't Worth Jack

I felt the raw energy and smashed clean through the ceiling. 5,000 miles up and climbing fast, I'm doing Mach 2. I stop dead at the sight of the moon. With this power, I could save the world. First things first.

Shooting across the globe three hundred feet off the deck and I'm heading for…..
"Damn."

I can't undo what's been done and for some reason, that's what I believe would do the most good. Stupid super powers ain't worth jack.

"Am I getting old?" I swear I would have done something cool with these powers when I was nine or ten. Oh well.

I felt the raw energy and smashed clean through the ceiling. 5,000 miles up and climbing fast, I'm doing Mach2. Breaking orbit, I laugh quietly to myself because I can breathe in space, I'm un-killable, and I'm going somewhere way better than this.

(Spring 2007)

A Good Reason to Buy Cereal

The jewel heist made all the papers. Not at first, but when the thieves were caught and the loot wasn't recovered, the story transgressed into infamy. The way I heard it; the cops chased them into a cereal factory.

There was a stand-off and finally, a shoot out. All this must've taken four, maybe five hours. Apparently the conveyor belts and packaging line were running the whole time. Just before the SWAT teams were tapped to assault; all the delivery trucks were removed from the facility perimeter. Cops would later cry S.O.P. on that.

Some lucky bastard somewhere went to pour a bowl of the "everyday" and came up 6.8 million dollars richer. Rubies and milk.

(2008)

Frontal Lobe Stew

I could feel the way of things becoming more and more negative in the rapidity of time. If I cannot find some way to regulate all the negativity I will crumble as sure as an old stone bridge will eventually fall away. Savannah is simply an open wound to be played with in a macabre style. Thoughts of her exhaust me as fast as anything I can think of. Think faster.

I want to be with her. I want to be poor and sleep with our baby in the bed with us. If I could sacrifice everything for such an arrangement I would.

God damn this life. Ecrasez!

I need to work this out, because if I can't my frontal lobe will leak out from my nose. That would be a sight to see, my heart and my frontal lobe in a bowl on the counter in the kitchen. Frontal lobe stew for me and you.

(2008)

TO: god

Build me a pyramid that I might lie under
when I die.

Give me a woman who, in my absence, will
cry.

Find me a place where the sun always
shines,

but rain falls as well.

If I live a hundred years and die a death that
had no fear -

A happy man you'll find me there.

Foresight

I ripped open time. Not on purpose. Because of this, I'm sure most things discovered, are discovered by accident.

Instead of saying, "hello", people should greet each other by announcing one real fact about their lifestyle or feelings. Try saying, "I'm gay", or "I eat cold pizza in the mornings." Substitute, "nice weather" with, "I feel my size imposes on people." Try "I hate paying for a war I didn't want to fight." Instead of, "did you see the game last night?"

I suggest this here because the future is so fucked up. If I was allowed, I would tell you all about it. I am not of course. Morality and humility do not permit me. When I fell into the newest uncharted time hole, I saw my future and yours. And I was aghast.

(June 2008)

One Date Wonder

A recipe for a bitter sweet concoction that will hardly satisfy and, is difficult to prepare. This rare dish has a full-bodied taste but produces a rather melancholy after effect.

1 28yr. old boy

1 21yr. old girl

1 stark admission by the boy, produced by a terrible story told by the girl. (at this point boy must have been marinating in thoughts of girl for at least a week)

1 guaranteed Friday get together (any other day of the week will not do)

24hrs. of panic and excitement

1 2hr. phone call w/ hope and compassion (boy tries to calm girl)

4-6 Lilies (from a flower shop run by a bitter woman)

2 drunk parents for light-hearted awkwardness

1 lousy Italian restaurant (must be an unplanned meal)

1 45.min foot rub

1 hr. of raw intimacy and the desire for nothing else

1 pair of sultry eyes (to convince a man anything is possible)

4 kisses, 2 good – 2 bad

14hrs. of consideration by girl

1 rather hasty decision

1 ambush style phone call

4 lies sprinkled liberally into phone call

Serve

From Monday to Monday

I had you in the palm of my hand.

You were exposed and vulnerable, and you can't deny it. Why didn't I take everything from you? That is, why didn't I take all that I wanted? Because I can't I can only take what I'm offered.

My life will be diminished permanently because I did not make love to you. But I know that you did not have to compromise yourself – and because of that I know I am a good man.

I cannot be so mad at you, because through you I found I could feel all those things again and still let you slip away.

(October 2010)

www.ingramcontent.com/pod-product-compliance
Ingram Content Group UK Ltd.
Pitfield, Milton Keynes, MK11 3LW, UK
UKHW020219250726
13967UKWH00001B/93

9 781300 869122